S0-AFG-908

MATT CHRISTOPHER®

#8
HEAD TO HEAD

Text by **Stephanie Peters**
Illustrated by **Michael Koelsch**

LITTLE, BROWN AND COMPANY

New York ⌁ Boston

Little, Brown and Company

Time Warner Book Group
1271 Avenue of the Americas, New York, NY 10020
Visit our Web site at www.lb-kids.com

www.mattchristopher.com

First Edition

The characters and events portrayed in this book are fictitious.
Any similarity to real persons, living or dead, is coincidental
and not intended by the author.

Matt Christopher® is a registered trademark
of Catherine M. Christopher.

Library of Congress Cataloging-in-Publication Data
Peters, Stephanie True.
Head to head / Matt Christopher ; text by Stephanie Peters ;
illustrated by Michael Koelsch. — 1st ed.
      p.   cm. — (The extreme team ; #8)
Summary: Mark finds that he is jealous when his friend Jonas
seems to learn kung fu much more quickly than he did.
ISBN 0-316-15581-0 (hc) / ISBN 0-316-15582-9 (pb)
[1. Kung fu — Fiction.   2. Jealousy — Fiction.
3. Self-perception — Fiction.]   I. Christopher, Matt.
II. Koelsch, Michael, ill.   III. Title.   IV. Series.
PZ7.P441833Hea 2004   2004008639
                    [Fic] — dc22

10   9   8   7   6   5   4   3   2   1

COM-MO (pb)

CHAPTER ONE

"Hey, hey! It's your birthday! Hey, hey! It's your birthday!"

Mark Goldstein heard his friends before he saw them. Xavier "X" McSweeney, Charlie Abbott, Savannah Smith, Belicia "Bizz" Juarez, and Jonas Malloy were singing at the top of their lungs as they trooped in to the kung-fu *kwoon* where Mark took lessons. He wasn't there for a lesson this Saturday, however. He was having his birthday party at the martial-arts school.

"Over here, guys!" Mark called. The kids greeted Mark's parents, then surrounded Mark.

"This is going to be awesome!" X said, rubbing his hands together.

"You bet it is." Sifu Eric Hale, Mark's teacher, came out of his office. He led the children to a large, open room with red mats on the floor and mirrors along one wall. He motioned for Mark to step forward.

"At our school," the teacher said, "more experienced students help out those just starting to learn kung fu. Today Mark is the one with experience and you are the beginners. All set, Mark?"

Mark got into the horse-riding stance — feet wide apart, toes pointed out, knees bent. He pulled his elbows tight into his sides, his fists turned upward.

"Four punches, left-side kick, right block, leg sweep," Sifu Hale said.

Mark's fists jabbed forward, one, two, one, two. His left leg flashed sideways. His right arm flew up to knock away an imaginary punch. He dropped to a crouch and swept his right leg around as if to trip an opponent. Then he hopped back up and returned to the horse-riding stance.

"That was totally fluid!" Jonas cried. The other kids laughed.

"Totally *what?*" Sifu Hale asked, smiling.

"Fluid. You know, smooth, like waves in one of those wave-machine things!" Jonas rolled his arms up and down.

As everyone laughed again, Mark glanced at his teacher. He knew Sifu Hale didn't like kids clowning around during class. *Of course, this isn't class, it's a party,* Mark reminded himself.

Sifu Hale interrupted them. "Actually, fluid is just what you want to be when practicing martial arts. Each move should flow into the next." He motioned for them to stand. "Okay, time for the rest of you to be fluid, too. Copy Mark's stance and try the punches first."

With Sifu Hale and Mark watching closely, the five friends did as instructed.

"Not bad," Sifu Hale said, "but, Bizz, put your thumbs on the outside of your fists. If you were really hitting something, they would be broken by now."

4

Bizz hurriedly shifted her thumbs to the correct position.

"I did the same thing the first time I tried punches," Mark admitted. She gave him a smile.

"Next move: the side kick," the teacher said. "Mark, show them again, in slow motion, please."

Mark went through the move in four parts: lifting his knee up in front of him to the chamber position, thrusting his leg out sideways, chambering it again, and putting his foot down. The others followed suit.

"Good. Practice a few more times, then try to put the punches and the kick together. Nice and slow, then pick up momentum," said Sifu Hale.

For the next few minutes, the room was silent except for the sound of cloth moving — and of X murmuring "punch, punch, punch, punch, kick, get ready" over and over.

Mark was doing the moves, too, when he heard Sifu Hale say, "Totally fluid, Jonas. You seem to have a knack for kung fu."

CHAPTER TWO

Mark looked at Jonas's reflection in the mirror. He tried to remember if his teacher had ever told him that he had a knack for kung fu. He was pretty sure he hadn't.

Jonas caught Mark watching him. He grinned and did the punch-kick combination — then added the arm block and the leg sweep. Each move was perfect. Mark looked away with a funny feeling in the pit of his stomach.

While they worked on the moves, Sifu Hale set up an obstacle course with tunnels, stacks of mats, and stationary punching bags. "Courses like this challenge you to quickly adapt your movements to new situations," Sifu Hale explained. "Let's see how you do."

One by one the kids crawled, hopped, and punched their way through the course. "I never knew it could feel so good to hit something!" Savannah cried as she pummeled the bag.

X held up his hands in mock terror. "Just so long as the bag's your target, and not me!" he joked.

Savannah struck a fighting pose. "Don't tempt me, X-man," she growled playfully, pretending to jab at him.

"I'll protect you, X!" Jonas bellowed. He jumped in between X and Savannah.

"My hero!" X trilled in a high voice.

As Mark watched his friends goof around, the knot in his stomach loosened. *So they don't take kung fu seriously,* he thought. *Big deal. They don't know what really goes on here.*

After they finished the obstacle course, Sifu Hale had everyone line up against the back wall. He took out a huge body ball and bounced it a few times.

"You kids have heard of dodgeball, right?" Before they could answer, he flung the ball toward Charlie and X. They darted out of the way and the ball hit the wall, bouncing back to the teacher. He hurled it again, this time at Bizz. She, too, got out of the way just in time. On the next throw, Charlie wasn't as quick and had to take a seat against the back wall.

They played three rounds of dodgeball. Bizz won the first round; Jonas, the next round; and Charlie, the third. Mark came in second each time.

"Okay, one more activity before you hit the party room," Sifu Hale said. He took out a long foam noodle, the kind used in swimming pools to help people float. He told the kids to get in a circle around him. "Let's see how quick your reflexes are. If the noodle taps you three times, you're out. Ready?"

He held the noodle at the height of their heads. "Crouch low like a snake in the grass!" He spun around. Laughing, the kids ducked to avoid being tapped.

"Now jump like a leopard pouncing!" This time Sifu Hale whipped the soft noodle around at floor

level. Savannah and X were too slow and got bumped, but the others cleared it. Sifu Hale continued to call "crouch!" and "jump!", tapping the slower players until at last there was a single person left in the circle — Jonas.

"To the one with the best reflexes goes the prize," the teacher said. He handed the noodle to Jonas and bowed. Jonas accepted the prize and returned the bow.

Like a fist to the gut the funny feeling returned to Mark's stomach.

CHAPTER THREE

The party ended soon after the cake and ice cream were gone. Mark's friends had given him a lot of cool presents and he made sure he thanked them all when it was time for everyone to head home.

Mr. and Mrs. Goldstein collected Mark's gifts. "We'll help you finish cleaning up after we put these in the car," his mother said.

Mark nodded. One of the *kwoon* rules was that students help keep the place clean. That meant party rooms, too, so after his parents left he picked up a broom and started sweeping.

"Happy birthday, Mark! Can I give you a hand?"

Mark looked up and was surprised to see Mr. Malloy. He thought Jonas had already left.

"Uh, no, but thanks anyway, Mr. Malloy," Mark replied. "I guess Jonas is around here somewhere."

"He's in there, talking with your teacher." Mr. Malloy jerked a thumb over his shoulder.

Mark looked into the office. Jonas was sitting across from Sifu Hale. As Mark watched, Jonas gathered up a pile of forms, shook Sifu Hale's hand, and walked out with a big grin on his face.

"What's going on?" Mark asked as Jonas joined them.

"I'll tell you what's going on!" Jonas fake punched Mark in the arm. "I'm signing up to take lessons. Say hello to your new kung-fu buddy!"

Mark nearly dropped the broom. "You — you're going to be taking lessons here?"

"Won't it be great? We can practice all our moves together. It'll be cool." Jonas tugged on his coat. "Hey, get back to your broom, bro. I want this place

spic and span for my first lesson on Monday!" He gave a wave and followed his father out the door.

"Yeah. Right." But Mark didn't immediately start sweeping. Instead, he closed his eyes and took slow, deep breaths. When he opened his eyes again, he felt better. He got to work.

Sifu Hale came out of his office. "Did you have a good time today, Mark?" he asked.

Mark nodded. "It was great, Sifu."

"Your friend Jonas has a lot of energy," Sifu Hale went on. "I'm sure he'll be able to use it when he starts next week."

Mark swept up the last of the cake crumbs and emptied the dustpan into the trash without saying a word. He could feel his teacher's eyes on him.

"Everything okay, Mark?"

"Everything's fine," he said.

His teacher started to leave the room, then turned back. "By the way, I'm having an open house here next month. You know, to show people in the community what our kung-fu school is all about. I need two students from each level to demonstrate differ-ent moves. Would you be interested in helping out?"

"Sure!" Mark said.

"Great. Have your parents stop in before you leave to sign the permission form. Then I'll call to let you know when practices are."

As Mark put the broom away and turned off the lights to the party room, his heart felt light again. *Well, what do you know!* he thought. *If he wants me in the demonstration, I must have some sort of knack for kung fu, after all!*

CHAPTER FOUR

Monday afternoon, Mark and Jonas got to the *kwoon* at the same time. Class began when all the other beginner students arrived.

Sifu Hale had them stretch out and do some jumping jacks to warm up. Then he broke them into two groups, one made up of new students, the other of advanced beginners. Jonas was in the first; Mark, in the second. Sifu Hale went through basic moves with Jonas's group. Another instructor ran Mark and his bunch through more complicated combinations.

Mark watched Jonas out of the corner of his eye. Sifu Hale corrected Jonas's position a few times, but after that Jonas seemed to do everything just right.

Mark tried not to remember how long it had taken him to learn those same moves. Even now he sometimes faltered.

At the end of class, Mark found a place to sit on the mats. This was his favorite part, the time when students were asked to close their eyes and quiet their minds. Usually he had no trouble doing that. But today, it took him longer because the person behind him kept fidgeting. He had finally managed to block out the noises when Sifu Hale announced that class was over.

Mark glanced behind him to identify the squirmer, but whoever it was had already gone.

Over the next few weeks, Mark was busy with homework and kung-fu lessons. His spare time was spent preparing for the demonstration. He was so wrapped up in those preparations that he didn't even have time to spend with his friends – except Jonas, of course, whom he saw at the *kwoon* regularly. Jonas was making great progress. In fact, his moves were better than those of a few students who had been taking lessons for months. That included Mark.

Other than Jonas, though, Mark didn't see much of anyone. On the Friday a week before the demonstration, X pulled Mark aside.

"Dude, you have been missed at the skatepark. Two weekends and no show! Come tomorrow morning, okay?"

"I will," Mark promised.

True to his word, Mark met up with his friends when the park opened at ten the next morning. Alison Lee, the teenager who supervised the park, bumped fists with him as he entered.

"My uncle Eric tells me you're in the demonstration at the school," she said. Sifu Hale was Alison's uncle. She had introduced him — and kung fu — to Mark back in September.

"You are?" Jonas was right behind Mark. "How come you didn't tell me?"

Mark just shrugged.

"Well, maybe later you can show me what you'll be doing for it."

Mark stepped onto his skateboard and kicked off. "Maybe," he said as he rolled away. *But don't plan on it,* he added silently. He knew Jonas would want to try the moves. And knowing Jonas, he'd be better at them.

The skatepark wasn't busy yet, which was fine with Mark. He wasn't the best boarder. And since he hadn't ridden for a few weeks, he was pretty sure he'd be worse than usual. So while most of his friends moved toward the ramps and rails, he decided to warm up on a flat surface first.

Helmet, wrist pads, and knee pads securely in place, Mark practiced boarding in one direction, spinning around on his back wheels, and then boarding back to his starting spot. Once that was going smoothly, he tried adding an ollie midway through the run. He landed the first few jumps easily. Feeling more confident, he attempted a kick flip. His board

popped up nice and high, but when he tried to spin it with his toe he caught the board wrong and fell.

As he picked himself up and dusted off his pants, he heard a *whoop* from the rails. He looked over to see Jonas ride a rail on his skateboard, land cleanly — and do a perfect kick flip.

"Figures," Mark muttered.

CHAPTER FIVE

Just then, Mark heard X call his name. He reluctantly boarded over to the rails.

"Savannah is about to do her first fifty-fifty grind!" X cried. He turned to Savannah and yelled, "Go for it, girl!"

Savannah stepped onto her skateboard and rode hard at a low rail. When she got close to the rail's end, she popped an ollie. The board's trucks landed squarely on the rail. Arms outstretched, Savannah slid down the rail's length. At the end she stuck a clean landing and boarded a few feet, then turned and stopped.

"Yes!" shouted Bizz.

"All right!" cheered Jonas.

"You did it!" cried Mark.

Savannah was grinning from ear to ear. "Bizz has been helping me all week. You should see the bumps and bruises I've got!"

"They can't be any worse than my paper cuts," Bizz said.

"Paper cuts? Why do you have paper cuts?" Mark asked.

"We're studying Japan in school and the teacher assigned us an origami project."

"What's origami?" X wanted to know.

"It's the ancient Japanese art of paper folding," Savannah explained. "You can make all kinds of cool things just by folding special paper the right way. It's easy."

Bizz snorted. "Maybe for you. For me, it's torture! If it weren't for your help, I'd still be trying to figure it out."

"Learning to do that grind was torture, too," Savannah admitted. "Well, now that I've done it, I'm ready for a drink break. Come on."

Mark joined them on the soft grass. He took off his pads and helmet, then grabbed a juice box from his backpack, stuck in the straw, and took a long drink.

"Hey, Mark and Jonas," X said suddenly, "show us what you've been doing in kung fu!"

Mark almost choked on his juice, but Jonas scrambled to his feet.

"Watch this!" he said. He got into the horse-riding stance. Then, with a blur of movement, he threw a series of punches, blocks, and kicks. Each move looked perfect.

X and the others applauded.

"Thank you, thank you," Jonas said, bowing theatrically. "Now, for my next trick, I need a volunteer from the audience." He held his hand out to Mark. "How about you, little boy?"

"Uh, I don't think so. Choose someone else," Mark mumbled.

Jonas shook his head. "No one else here knows kung fu," he said. "I wanted to show them how we spar with partners. C'mon!"

"Yeah, c'mon, Mark!" the others urged.

Even though he really didn't want to, Mark got to his feet. "You know, you've only been doing kung fu for a few weeks," he said. "I'm not sure you're ready to spar."

"What, are you chicken, or something?" Jonas said with a grin.

Mark glared at Jonas. "No. I'm just saying it might not be smart. But if you really want to . . ."

Jonas and Mark stood face to face and bowed. They both got into a fighting stance called the snake. Their feet pointed sideways, but their upper bodies were turned toward one another. They raised their arms chest high with their hands flat.

"Ready?" Jonas asked. Mark nodded.

Jonas came at Mark with a right-hand punch. Mark blocked it cleanly, but before he knew what was happening Jonas tapped him in the ribs with his left hand. "Gotcha!" Jonas cried.

Mark turned crimson. He wanted to quit right then, but instead he got back into the snake stance. This time he attacked Jonas with three punches. But Jonas was too quick for him. He blocked every punch and danced out of range. "Can't get me!" he taunted.

Mark felt his frustration grow. To get himself under control, he closed his eyes and took a deep breath — just as Jonas lunged forward.

CHAPTER SIX

"Oof!"

Mark staggered back a step, clutching his middle.

"Oh, man, Mark, I am so sorry!" Jonas's eyes were wide. "I thought you were ready!"

"Guess I wasn't," Mark gasped. He turned and started putting on his skateboard gear.

"Is everything okay?" Jonas asked anxiously. "You're not really hurt, right?"

"I'm fine," Mark said. "I just remembered that I have to get going." He could feel his friends staring at him as he stepped onto his board and shoved off, but he didn't look back. He was afraid that if he did, they might notice the tears brimming in his eyes.

When Mark got home, he crept up to his room, closed the door, and flopped down on his bed. He was still in that position when his mother knocked on his door half an hour later.

"So you are here!" she said. "I didn't hear you come home. Sifu Hale called earlier to ask you to stop by the school for some demo practice. Can you be ready to go in fifteen minutes?"

"Sure, Mom," he replied. But he didn't move.

"Is everything okay, honey?" his mother asked. She sounded worried.

Mark sighed and rolled off the bed. "Yeah, everything's fine."

Twenty minutes later, his mother dropped him off at the school. "I'll pick you up in half an hour," she said. She looked at him closely. "Unless you want me to come sooner?"

"A half hour's fine," Mark said reassuringly.

Inside, the other students taking part in the demonstration were doing their warm-ups. As Mark waved to some and bumped fists with others, his bad mood started to melt away. By the time he was through with his stretches he felt calm.

After warm-ups, Sifu Hale reviewed the sequence of events that would happen on the day of the demonstration. Students would take turns showing the audience what they were learning. Mark and his partner, Jenna, would first do a series of basic moves. Then they would demonstrate simple throws where one person pretended to attack the other but got tossed to the mat instead. Older, more experienced students would spar, and the most advanced would demonstrate how to use swords and spears. Mark looked forward to a time when he could use such weapons, but he knew he had much to learn before he was ready for that.

Jenna and Mark stood side by side and began to run through their set. Sifu Hale had asked that they do their moves slowly so that the audience could see each one clearly. Mark was so focused that he paid no attention to Jenna — until his teacher asked her a question.

"Jenna," Sifu Hale said, "are you limping?"

Mark stopped short and stared at his partner.

"Yes," Jenna mumbled. "I twisted my ankle this morning. But I'm fine!"

"I'll be the judge of that," Sifu Hale said. "Sit, please." He examined her ankle. It was swollen and black and blue, and it looked very painful.

"Jenna, this is badly sprained." Sifu Hale helped Jenna to a bench. "I'm sorry, but I'm afraid you're out of the demonstration."

"But I won't have a partner for the throws!" Mark blurted out. The minute he said it he wished he could put the words back in his mouth. Jenna had looked simply disappointed before, but now she looked guilty *and* disappointed.

Sifu Hale stood up. "I'll see if I can find someone to take Jenna's place. Meantime, Mark, can you get an ice pack?"

Mark was wrapping the pack in a towel when the door to the school opened and Jonas walked in.

"Good, you're here!" he said when he spotted Mark. "Listen, I —"

"Jonas!" Sifu Hale came out of his office. "Just the boy I wanted to see. How would you like to take Jenna's place in the demonstration?"

The ice pack slipped from Mark's hands and fell to the floor with a crash.

CHAPTER SEVEN

"But, Sifu, the demo's in a week," Jonas said. "Do you really think I can learn everything I have to do by then?"

"You can if you put your mind to it," Sifu Hale said. He glanced up at the clock. "I'm afraid practice is over for today, however. There's an adult class coming in. Mark, do you think you might be able to show Jonas the set at home?"

Mark knelt down to pick up the pack. "Sure," he mumbled. "Let me get this to Jenna first." He hurried out of the hallway and back into the studio.

"Whoa, what happened? You look more bummed

out than I do." Jenna reached for the ice pack. "Is everything okay?"

"*Yes!*" Mark suddenly exploded. "Man, you're, like, the tenth person who's asked me that today!"

Jenna pulled her hand back with a hurt look. Mark immediately felt bad about his outburst. "Sorry," he said. "And I'm sorry about your ankle, too."

Jenna opened her mouth to say something, but she didn't get the chance.

"Hey, Mark, I'm ready when you are!" Jonas bounded into the studio and struck a fighting pose.

Jenna's eyes went from him to Mark and back again. "My substitute?" she asked.

Mark nodded.

Jenna sighed. "That was quick."

"Quick?" Jonas echoed. "You want to see quick? I'll show you quick!" His arms punched the air eight times. "Now *that* was quick!"

Jenna rolled her eyes. "I think I hear my mom calling," she said, sliding off the bench and hobbling into the hall. "See you, Mark. Bye, Jonas." Mark waved good-bye, but Jonas was busy watching himself do blocks in the mirror.

"I can't believe Sifu Hale asked me to be in the demo," Jonas said. "Is that cool, or what?"

"Yeah, real cool. Listen, we should get going if we're going to have time to practice before dinner."

"Sure thing," Jonas said. "Let's go outside and tell your mom to pick you up at my house in an hour. My dad can drive us home and we can practice in my basement, okay?"

Mark's mother agreed to pick him up at Jonas's house. Ten minutes later, the boys were in the Malloys' basement.

Mark stood in front of Jonas. "I guess we should warm up first," he said.

"Nah. I'm ready already." Jonas hopped from foot to foot impatiently. "C'mon, just show me the moves!"

Mark sighed. "All right." He got into the horse-riding stance. From there he moved forward slowly, one foot at a time, blocking first with one arm, then the other. Next he turned to one side and threw two punches.

"Now you try," he said, returning to his starting point.

"Piece of cake," Jonas said. He held the stance for a moment, then shot forward like he was speed skating and jerked his arms up into the blocks. He spun and jabbed out the punches. "How was that?"

CHAPTER EIGHT

Mark wasn't sure what to say. Jonas had done the moves just fine, but much faster than Mark had shown them. "Um, that was good, except Sifu Hale wants us to do the stuff slowly."

Jonas crossed his arms over his chest. "Are you kidding? None of the other students in the demo are moving slow, are they?" Mark shook his head. "I'll bet Sifu Hale just doesn't think we can do our stuff fast. It's up to us to show him we can! I guarantee you he'll be psyched when he sees us. And the audience will totally love it, too! So I say, let's do it fast and surprise him."

Since Jonas wasn't listening to anything he said,

Mark didn't bother to explain why they were supposed to go slow. He simply got into starting position.

Jonas did, too. Mark called out the moves one by one. Blocks, punches, kicks, stances — Jonas whipped off each one with precision and speed. Next to him, Mark felt clumsy and awkward. And all the while, the same questions nagged at him: What if Jonas was right? What if the real reason Sifu Hale had told Mark to do the moves slowly was because he didn't think he could do them at full speed? What if his teacher had asked Jonas to be Jenna's sub because he knew Jonas would do everything right?

With these thoughts whirling in his brain, Mark lost his concentration. He flubbed the set halfway through and had to start from the beginning again. It didn't help that Jonas watched him as he worked painstakingly through each move.

When he finally got it right, Mark was exhausted. He was more than ready to leave Jonas's house — and Jonas.

"One more time, okay?" Jonas said.

Mark groaned. "Not right now, Jonas. I'm beat," he said. "Besides, my mom will be here any minute."

"So let's use that time to practice some more. C'mon, what do you say?" Jonas stepped toward Mark and elbowed him playfully in the ribs. "C'mon, c'mon, c'mon."

"Jonas, cut it out."

Jonas kicked Mark lightly, then bobbed away. "C'mon, what are you afraid of?" he said. He nudged Mark with his foot again.

Suddenly, Mark grabbed Jonas's leg with both his hands. Still holding the leg, he spun away from Jonas on one foot. His other foot swung around and connected with Jonas's standing leg.

"*Yow!*" Jonas cried as he fell to the floor in a heap. He stared up at his friend in shock. "What — what was that?"

Mark picked up his backpack and slung it over his shoulder. "That was a preview of the next lesson." Without another word, he walked up the stairs and

out the door. When his mother rolled into the drive-way a moment later, Mark didn't even look back to see if Jonas had followed him.

"How did Jonas do?" his mother asked as they drove home. "Were you able to teach him what he needed to know?"

Mark thought about Jonas lying on the floor. A small, satisfied smile crept across his face. "You know, Mom, I think maybe I did."

CHAPTER NINE

After breakfast the next morning, Mark decided to head for the skatepark. Even though it had felt good at the time, now he was feeling a little guilty for how he had surprised Jonas the day before. He figured Jonas would be at the park and he could explain why he'd done what he did.

But when he arrived, Savannah was the only one there.

"Where is everybody?" he asked.

"Let's see." Savannah ticked off each friend on her fingers. "Bizz is finishing her origami project. X is at his brother's baseball game. Charlie had to help his dad around the house. I thought Jonas would be here, but I haven't seen him yet."

Mark didn't say anything, but he had a pretty good idea why Jonas hadn't shown up.

"So it's just you and me," Savannah said, "which means I can take it nice and easy instead of doing all those tricks Bizz is always trying to get me to do."

Mark adjusted his helmet. "Don't you like learning those things?"

Savannah shrugged. "Oh, sure, sometimes I do. But other times, it makes me feel bad — and I'm not just talking about the bruises I get from falling." She fiddled with her elbow pads before going on. "If you want to know the truth, sometimes I'm jealous of Bizz. She's so good at sports and stuff. You know what I mean?"

Mark knew exactly what she meant. How could he not? He'd been feeling the same thing about Jonas for weeks now.

Savannah stood up and stepped onto her board. "Well, what do you say? Ready to roll?"

Mark kicked off. "Nice and easy!"

He was still thinking about what Savannah had said about being jealous when he entered the *kwoon* that afternoon for another practice session. Jonas was already there. As Mark watched him fool around with some of the other students, someone laid a hand on his shoulder.

"How did Jonas do yesterday?" Sifu Hale asked.

"He did great," Mark admitted.

"Good," Sifu Hale said, nodding. "He certainly seems to have learned the moves quickly. Now if he can just learn the other part of kung fu, he'll be well on his way."

Mark turned to look at his teacher. "What do you mean, 'other part'?"

Sifu Hale didn't answer. Instead, he motioned Mark into his office. When they were both sitting down, he leaned across the desk. "Your friend Jonas is very coordinated, and he's a fast learner. But so far kung fu, for him, is all about kicking and punching. He hasn't begun to learn the other stuff, focus and

discipline. He's barely able to control himself long enough to sit still during the five-minute meditation each class. Until he does, he won't go far in martial arts."

Mark flashed back to the person whose squirming had bothered him. Now he realized that it could have been Jonas.

Sifu Hale smiled at him. "Do you know why I chose you for the demonstration?"

Mark shook his head.

"It's not because your moves are perfect. They're not. But with practice, they'll get better." The teacher steepled his fingers. "When you do kung fu, Mark, your focus shows in your face. I can tell just by looking at you that you are concentrating fully. It takes a lot to distract you. I think the audience will be able to see that. That's why I chose you — to show people how important focus is to kung fu. And perhaps," he added, standing up and coming around the desk, "there are others who could learn by watching you, too."

CHAPTER TEN

Mark left the office feeling better than he had in days. Only one thing was still bothering him, and he knew just how to get rid of it.

He marched into the studio and up to Jonas. "I need to talk to you." He pulled Jonas to a bench. "I'm sorry about tripping you yesterday," he said. "You weren't ready for it. It was unfair."

Jonas gave a sheepish grin. "Well, I may not have been ready for it, but you know what? I deserved it! I was acting like a jerk at my house. At the skatepark, too, actually. That's why I showed up here yesterday — to apologize for making you spar me."

Mark grinned back. "While we're busy apologizing,

I better say I'm sorry for giving you the cold shoulder at the skatepark. I — I guess I've been a little jealous of how quickly you've picked up kung fu. You do the moves way better than I do. I wish there was a way I could do them as well."

They sat in silence for a moment. Then Mark stood up. "So, you wanna get practicing?"

Jonas caught his sleeve. "Wait. There's something else."

Mark sat back down. "What?"

"You say you're jealous of my moves, right? Well, I'm a little jealous of you, too. I wish I had as much self-control as you do. But man, it's the hardest thing in the world for me to sit still after class." He looked at Mark. "Do you think maybe we could help each other out somehow?"

Mark remembered Sifu Hale's words: *Perhaps there are others who could learn by watching you.* Mark wondered if Sifu Hale had meant Jonas. Then he realized it didn't matter. Jonas was asking for his help, and Mark hoped he'd be able to give it.

And who knows? he thought. *Maybe I can learn from watching Jonas, too.*

The following week, Mark and Jonas worked every afternoon to prepare for the demonstration. But before their first session, Mark made sure he explained why Sifu Hale wanted them to do the moves slowly.

"Oh, that makes sense," Jonas said. And that was that.

Sifu Hale had decided Mark and Jonas would do just one throw instead of the three Mark and Jenna had been scheduled to demonstrate.

"Will you be able to learn it in time, Jonas?" the teacher asked.

Jonas glanced at Mark and grinned. "Oh, I think so. I've already had a preview. I'm looking forward to trying it out, myself!"

And learn it he did — Mark had the bruises to show for it. But that was okay, because he was pretty sure Jonas had a few new black and blues as well.

The day of the demonstration, they sat together

in the party room with the other students, listening to the murmurs from the gathering audience.

"Sounds like a lot of people out there," Jonas commented suddenly. "I hope I don't screw up."

Mark looked at him in surprise. "You're not nervous, are you?" he said.

Jonas made a small space between his thumb and forefinger. "Maybe just a little."

"Well, you know what to do, then," Mark told him.

Jonas nodded, closed his eyes, and took several deep breaths. After a moment, he opened his eyes again and smiled. "That's such a neat trick. Thanks again for showing it to me."

"No sweat," Mark said. He heard Sifu Hale call their names. "Now, let's go show those folks what kung fu is all about!"

The Animal Stances of Kung Fu

The martial art of kung fu began hundreds of years ago in a monastery in China. The monks there learned hand-fighting techniques so that they could protect their monastery from invaders. Many of these techniques are based on the movements of five animals: the snake, the tiger, the crane, the leopard, and the mythical Chinese dragon.

The snake is a legless, armless creature. It moves silently, almost invisibly. When it defends itself, it coils its body, and its head rises straight out of the coil. Its strikes are sudden, so it is hard to see them coming. Snake moves in kung fu mimic those made by real snakes. Arms and legs bend like the letter *s*. Lightning-fast strikes are made with the fingertips, which are held like fangs and target soft areas of the body.

The tiger is a powerful, aggressive animal. It attacks head on with great ferocity, using its huge paws and strong jaws to overwhelm its prey. Tigers rarely need to defend themselves, and tiger kung-fu moves are mostly attack based, too, with fierce kicks and punches but few blocks.

The leopard uses stealth, cunning, and agility to surprise its prey. Kung-fu moves based on this animal share these qualities: fighters attack in unexpected ways and catch their opponents off guard using their quickness.

The crane is a graceful, patient bird. Unlike the tiger and the leopard, it is not aggressive — but if it has to, it will use its claws, sharp beak, and powerful wings to defend itself. Crane kung-fu techniques are likewise based on grace and patience. Fighters using crane techniques always let their opponents attack first before fighting back.

The Chinese dragon is a mythical creature believed to bring good luck and prosperity. It is the most spiritual of the five kung-fu animals. People who study dragon techniques focus on building their inner strength as well as their bodily strength. When they fight, they use open hands held like claws for grabbing their opponents.

There are other animals associated with martial arts, including the praying mantis, the monkey, and the eagle. If you can imagine how each of these creatures looks and moves, then you may be able to guess how their traits have been adapted to fighting and defense.

#1 ONE SMOOTH MOVE

#2 DAY OF THE DRAGON

#3 ROLLER HOCKEY RUMBLE

#4 ON THIN ICE

#5 ROCK ON

#6 INTO THE DANGER ZONE

#7 WILD RIDE

#8 HEAD TO HEAD